DISNEP
CLUB PENGUIN™

PICK YOUR PATH 2

The Inventor's Apprentice

CLUB PENGUIN™

PICK YOUR PATH 2

The Inventor's Apprentice

by Tracey West

Grosset & Dunlap

GROSSET & DUNLAP
Published by the Penguin Group
Penguin Group (USA) Inc., 375 Hudson Street, New York,
New York 10014, USA
Penguin Group (Canada), 90 Eglinton Avenue East, Suite 700,
Toronto, Ontario M4P 2Y3, Canada
(a division of Pearson Penguin Canada Inc.)
Penguin Books Ltd., 80 Strand, London WC2R 0RL, England
Penguin Group Ireland, 25 St. Stephen's Green, Dublin 2, Ireland
(a division of Penguin Books Ltd.)
Penguin Group (Australia), 250 Camberwell Road, Camberwell,
Victoria 3124, Australia
(a division of Pearson Australia Group Pty. Ltd.)
Penguin Books India Pvt. Ltd., 11 Community Centre, Panchsheel Park,
New Delhi—110 017, India
Penguin Group (NZ), 67 Apollo Drive, Rosedale,
North Shore 0632, New Zealand
(a division of Pearson New Zealand Ltd.)
Penguin Books (South Africa) (Pty.) Ltd., 24 Sturdee Avenue,
Rosebank, Johannesburg 2196, South Africa

Penguin Books Ltd., Registered Offices:
80 Strand, London WC2R 0RL, England

Library of Congress Cataloging-in-Publication Data is available.

ISBN 978-0-448-45037-7   10 9 8 7 6

Plink, plink, plink, plink.

You drop your *mancala* pebbles in holes around the game board. One of the pebbles lands in an empty hole opposite your opponent's side of the board.

"Capture!" you cry happily. The three pebbles in that hole drop into your *mancala*.

You tap your flipper to the beat of the funky music piped into the top floor of the Coffee Shop. Your opponent is a good friend of yours. She always beats you at *mancala*. But this time, you're going to win . . .

"Capture!" your friend shouts. You see five of your pebbles drop into her *mancala*. The game is over!

"Good game," you say as you collect your coins. "Want to play again?"

"Sure," your friend replies. But before you can sit back down at the game table, you get a postcard.

"Hold on," you say. "I've got a message."

You look at the postcard and see a picture of none other than Gary the Gadget Guy. Your heart beats faster as you read the card.

"Check this out!" you say. You read the message out loud.

"Congratulations! You are the winner of the Club Penguin Invention Contest! Your prize is a twenty-four-hour apprenticeship with me, Gary. We will begin at exactly 10:00 PST. Directions to my workshop will be sent in a separate postcard."

"Wow!" your friend says. "You get to meet Gary in person?"

"I can't believe it!" you say. You feel like jumping up and down with excitement.

You were so excited when you read about the Invention Contest. Gary announced it in the newspaper. He asked penguins to design an invention that would amp up one of the games on Club Penguin to make it more extreme. The only thing you like better than inventing is eating pizza, so you decided to enter.

You mailed Gary your plans for a freeze ray. You love playing ice hockey. With a freeze ray, you could turn patches of the sled-racing hill into ice so you could sled faster!

You never thought you'd win. You never win at anything—until now!

You glance at your watch. "Yikes! It's almost ten," you say. "I'd better go. I want to stop at my igloo and get the freeze ray I made."

"Meet me when your apprenticeship is over," your friend says. "I want to hear every detail!"

"You got it!" you promise.

You race to your igloo. It's a cold day, and you're glad you're wearing your favorite turtleneck and fuzzy snow boots. Inside your igloo, you quickly feed your yellow puffle, Einstein. Then you stuff the freeze ray into your messenger bag. Before you leave, you receive another postcard.

You'll find my workshop at the bottom of a hill, in a place where sports fans can get their fill.

It's the riddle from Gary! You study the first line. The hill must be the Ski Hill. There are two buildings at the bottom—the Ski Lodge and the Winter Sport Shop. You know where Gary's workshop is!

Snow crunches under your boots as you waddle up to the Sport Shop—the place where sports fans can get their fill. You are climbing up the stairs when you hear a voice behind the door.

"I see you've found my workshop! Good work, apprentice!"

7

You turn and find yourself face-to-face with Gary!

He looks exactly like his picture: blue, wearing a white lab coat. His round eyeglasses are so thick, you can't see the eyes behind them.

"Gary, I can't believe it's you! I am your biggest fan! I am so happy I won the contest! I worked really hard on my invention. So, does my apprenticeship start now? What do I do? Do I get to make inventions with you? Do I—"

Gary smiles and holds up a flipper to stop you. "I can see that you are excited. Enthusiasm and passion are trademarks of any good inventor. It's exactly what I'm looking for," he says. "Follow me."

Gary leads you inside the Sport Shop.

"There's no shortage of work to be done or contraptions to invent," he tells you. "I mentioned this to Aunt Arctic and she suggested I get an apprentice—someone to help me with my many inventions. It was such a good idea, I wish I had thought of it myself."

"I am ready to do whatever you want, Gary," you say.

"Perhaps we should begin with a tour of my

workshop," Gary suggests. "Then I can show you some of the inventions I've been working on."

That sounds great to you. Then you remember the freeze ray in your bag. You can't wait to show it to Gary! But you're worried that might not be polite. You wonder if you should wait until Gary gives you his tour first.

If you decide to wait to show Gary your freeze ray, go to page 17.
If you interrupt Gary and show him your freeze ray, go to page 31.

"It certainly is," Gary answers. "I have always been fascinated with the science behind surfing. I've been experimenting with rocket power to see if I can give *Catchin' Waves* a bit of a boost."

"Awesome," you agree. You examine the surfboard. There are two small rockets on the back of the board. They're attached to some kind of fuel tank with a small switch on top.

"I need you to test this out for me," Gary says, and you can't believe your luck.

"Will do! I'll come back with a full report," you promise.

"Excellent," Gary says. "I have arranged for you to test this out at the Cove. Please change into a wet suit and report back to me."

You quickly don the wet suit in a changing room. When you come out, you see a blue penguin wearing a red bathing suit, red sunglasses—and a jet pack. He's standing by the open shop door, ready to fly you to the Cove.

"Hey, Gary," he says. "All ready?"

"Absolutely," Gary replies. He hands you

the surfboard. "This invention is top secret. Test it out, but don't let anyone see you."

The blue penguin grabs you, and the two of you fly off. You start to panic.

"Gary, how do I work this thing?" you call down to Gary, who is watching you from the ground. But he can't hear you.

You fly over the Town Center, over the Snow Forts, over the Forest—and then the Cove is in sight below. You grip the board as the penguin flies you over the waves.

"Surf's up!" he cries.

Then you drop. But you're confused. You reach back to try to turn on the rockets. You don't see it coming, but a big wave is headed your way!

Wipe out! The wave pushes you back to shore. You jump up. Luckily, you're still holding the surfboard.

"Hey! What are you doing here?"

It's your friend. You try to hide the surfboard behind your back, but it's too big, of course. Your friend's eyes get wide.

"Is that one of Gary's new inventions?" she asks excitedly.

You start to tell her about the surfboard, then stop. Gary said it was top secret. You're not sure what to do. She is your *best* friend, after all.

If you tell your friend, go to page 53.
If you don't tell your friend,
go to page 76.

CONTINUED FROM PAGE 37.

Luckily, you land safely in an empty coffee cup. Not so luckily, the penguin holding the cup spots you.

"There's something weird in my cup!" he screams.

Panicked, he tosses the cup in the air. You go flying. You land safely again—this time, in the blond pigtails of an orange penguin. Unlike the last penguin, she doesn't seem to notice you. You grip one of her pigtails and hope you won't fall off.

The orange penguin leaves the Coffee Shop. She walks next door to the Night Club.

Once you're inside, the pounding music is so loud you have to hold your flippers over your ears. The colorful light-up dance floor is crowded with penguins. A bunch of them are doing a synchronized dance. The orange penguin gets on the floor and begins to dance along with them.

"Whoaaa!" You start to tumble around in her pigtails. You roll to the edge and grab on to a hair, but it's slippery. You lose your grip and fall to the dance floor.

You manage to land on both feet. But you have another problem. You are surrounded by stomping, tapping, dancing feet. Can you get out of the Night Club without getting squished?

Go to page 45.

CONTINUED FROM PAGE 20.

You press the triangle-shaped button.
Nothing happens.

Maybe this first row of buttons isn't powered up, you guess. You see that right above the square- and triangle-shaped buttons are a round button and a star-shaped button—and they're both blinking. The only trouble is, you still can't reach them.

You climb down from the shoe box and start searching around for something to give you a boost. Luckily, Gary is not the neatest penguin on the island. There are a bunch of items on the floor that could be useful. You almost pick up a coiled spring, but it looks like it could be dangerous. You settle on a spoon, a spool of thread, and a marble. The spoon is taller than you, and the marble is the size of your head.

You drag them all to the shoe box. You toss up the marble. You climb up and pull up the spoon. Then you climb down and try to lift up the spool of thread. It's so heavy! It's really exhausting being tiny.

Finally, you arrange the spoon and spool to

make a sort of seesaw. You stand on the handle of the spoon. Then you pick up the marble. You throw it onto the bowl of the spoon.

Whoosh! Your plan works, and you go shooting up into the air. The round- and star-shaped buttons are within reach. But which one should you push?

If you press the round button, go to page 41.
If you press the star-shaped button, go to page 21.

CONTINUED FROM PAGE 9.

You decide to show Gary your freeze ray later. You're anxious to see his workshop, anyway.

"Lead the way, Gary," you say.

You follow Gary past the exercise machine to the back wall of the Sport Shop. It's pretty messy. Blueprints of Gary's inventions are crookedly tacked to the wall. You spot the plans for the jet pack, the jackhammer, and others. Your flippers start to tingle with excitement.

This is where it all starts, you think.

The desk where Gary works is covered with papers and coffee stains. Metal springs, bolts, and other spare invention pieces are scattered on the floor. Papers spill out of a bulging file cabinet. Crumpled papers surround a blue recycling bin, but none of them have hit their target. Gary grabs a steaming cup of coffee from the desk and takes a sip.

Next to the desk is a hulking object covered by a blue tarp.

"Is that a new invention you're working on?" you ask, pointing.

"Oops! I should have put that somewhere safe," Gary replies. He rushes over to it and makes sure the tarp is secure. "You are one observant penguin. It will serve you well in this line of work. An inventor's work can't always be shared until it is ready. I'm afraid this project is still top secret."

You feel disappointed. You would love a peek at one of Gary's top secret projects.

"Let's see, where should we start?" Gary says. "Ah, yes, my desk. This is where all my ideas start. It usually takes several weeks for me to plan an invention."

You nod. "Yeah, it took me a long time to design my freeze ray," you agree.

"And these are my blueprints," Gary says, pointing to the wall, but something else catches your eye.

You hadn't noticed it before, somehow. But there's a door on the wall marked "Gary's Room." You are curious.

"Can we go in there?" you ask.

Gary adjusts his eyeglasses nervously. "Oh, I'm sorry, but that is not possible. The inventions behind that door are top secret."

Top secret. You like the sound of that. If only Gary would let you in!

The Sport Shop phone rings. Gary waddles over to answer it. He listens, nodding.

"That is not ideal," he says. "Don't worry. I'll be right there."

Gary hangs up the phone. "There is trouble with the Pizzatron 3000. This might be an excellent opportunity for you to learn machine repair. I must get to the Pizza Parlor right away. Would you like to come with me?"

You are about to say yes when you stop yourself. If you can convince Gary to let you stay in the Sport Shop, you might be able to peek at what's under that tarp. Or even try to open the top secret door.

You quickly shake the thought from your head. You couldn't do that—could you?

If you stay behind so you can check out Gary's secrets, go to page 34.
If you go with Gary to the Pizza Parlor, go to page 43.

CONTINUED FROM PAGE 63.

You decide you'd like to fix things before Gary finds out. One of those buttons must be able to turn you back to the right size. Science is all about experimentation, isn't it? You owe it to science to test it out for yourself.

First you have to reach the buttons. You spot a shoe box on the floor nearby. You go over and give it a push. Luckily, it's empty. But it's still a lot of work for a miniature penguin. Puffing and panting, you push the box across the floor and stop underneath the machine. Then you climb on top of it.

There are two buttons right in front of you: a square one and a triangle-shaped one. Which one should you push first?

If you push the square button, go to page 58.
If you push the triangle-shaped button, go to page 15.

CONTINUED FROM PAGE 16.

You press the star-shaped button.

Zap! A blue beam shoots from the laser. You dive off the shoe box to make sure the laser hits you.

Your body starts to tingle. You look down. You're starting to grow!

"That's a relief," you say. But then you notice something else.

Your color is starting to change. A pattern of red, white, and green plaid is popping up all over your body. You stop growing when you hit your normal size, but you are now plaid. You waddle to the Sport Shop mirror to get a good look at yourself.

"Ah, you have discovered the Size-a-Tron 3000."

You turn to see that Gary is back in the Sport Shop.

"I'm so sorry," you say. "I was just so curious."

Gary nodded. "I understand. Curiosity is a healthy trait for any inventor. Now let's get back to your apprenticeship."

"But I'm *plaid,*" you say. "Can you change me back?"

Gary shakes his head. "Unfortunately, I haven't figured out how to reverse the plaid ray," he says. "You should be back to normal in a few weeks or so."

"A few weeks?" You suddenly feel the urge to put on every item of clothing you own. "I'll be right back."

You rush off to your igloo, hoping no one will notice you. But of course that's impossible. Penguins start to crowd around you.

"Cool pattern!"

"Is that in the new Penguin Style catalog?"

"Hey, you look like a couch!"

Okay, so not everyone loves your new look. But you like the attention. You turn around and take your plaid self back to the Sport Shop. You have an apprenticeship to finish!

THE END

You bring the surfboard back to Gary.

"The rockets worked great in the beginning," you tell him. "But then the rockets went out. I think splashing water put them out."

"I thought that might happen," Gary says.

He waddles over to a big box next to his desk and rummages around in it. "Here they are."

He takes out two pieces of clear plastic.

"I designed these two rocket shields, but I worried they might get in the way of the rocket," he tells you. "However, now I think some kind of shield is necessary. Which shield would you like to test first? One is lightweight, and one is heatproof."

You hold each shield. Heatproof sounds like a good idea, but it feels very heavy. You wonder if it will slow down the surfboard.

If you test the lightweight shield, go to page 64.
If you test the heatproof shield, go to page 39.

CONTINUED FROM PAGE 75.

"Send me to the future!" you say boldly. "I want to go where no penguin has gone before."

Gary opens the curtain. "Please, step inside."

You obey. The walls inside the booth are lined with twisted tubes filled with neon-colored liquid.

"Cool," you say. Then you have a thought. "Hey, has this ever been tested before?"

"Yes," Gary says. "But not with anything alive."

That doesn't sound promising, but you're not about to back out. Gary closes the curtain.

"I will program your coordinates using a wireless control panel," he tells you. "Then I will activate the machine."

You hear Gary fidget with the control panel. Then he begins a countdown.

"Three . . . two . . . one . . ."

The machine begins to shake. The liquid in the tubes begins to swish and swirl. Then it starts to glow! The glowing neon light spirals around the tiny booth, making you dizzy. There is a faint buzzing in your ears. The next thing you see is a strange tunnel of dim light opening up in front of you, out of nowhere. Without warning, you feel yourself being sucked inside!

Suddenly, everything stops. You blink and realize you are inside the machine, but everything's quiet. Your journey must be over!

You step through the curtain. You are back in Gary's workshop, and Gary is standing right in front of you. "Greetings!" you tell him. "I am a penguin traveler from the past!"

"Yes, I know," he says. "Your test was successful! Welcome to the future."

"Awesome!" you say. "So, what's new on Club Penguin? Any new igloo designs? Is there a cool new party going on?"

Gary chuckles. "I am afraid you have only traveled twenty-three hours into the future," he tells you. "Things are very much the same as yesterday, except that you probably have a very hungry puffle waiting for you in your igloo."

"Oh, I forgot about Einstein! I'd better get home and feed it," you say.

"Wait!" Gary exclaims. "Before you go, have this."

Gary waddles over to his desk and reaches into a drawer. He takes something out and hands it to you.

"Here," he says. "A token of my thanks."

You look down and see a certificate in your hand. It reads "Official Inventor's Apprenticeship." You feel better already. You can't wait to hang it up in your igloo and show all of your friends!

THE END

CONTINUED FROM PAGE 46.

You decide to hitch a ride with the purple penguin. You wait until he walks past you and then you jump up onto his boot. You grab on to the laces. He throws one more snowball, then waves good-bye to the green penguin.

You feel like cheering as he heads down the path toward the Plaza.

"Pizza! Pizza!" you whisper, but he has other ideas. He steps inside the Pet Shop.

There are no other penguins in the shop. The first thing you notice is the playpen filled with puffles. They are huge! They're twice as tall as you, and their mouths look . . . well . . . big enough to swallow you up.

You look up at the purple penguin, hoping he'll get moving. He takes a blue device out of the pocket of his coat and starts fiddling with it. The next instant—poof! He's gone. And you're left sitting on the ground.

You're not sure what happened. But you don't have time to think about that now. The puffles in the pen seem very interested in you. Above the pen you see a curious red puffle on top of a post. The red puffle hops down to the ground. Now it is hopping toward you.

You run to the doors, but they're too heavy to budge. You turn and look at the red puffle. It's smiling. Maybe it just wants to be friends.

At least you hope that's what it wants. You've never read the ingredients on a box of Puffle-Os, but you're pretty sure puffles are vegetarians.

Right?

THE END

CONTINUED FROM PAGE 77.

You decide to try to fix it yourself, to impress Gary. You give it some thought. If water is splashing up and putting out the rocket flames, you need some kind of shield to keep the flames dry.

You look around on the shore. There's lots of snow, a plastic pail, some seashells . . .

You pick up the pail. It could work as a shield to keep the water off of the rocket flames. You just have to make sure you don't put the plastic too close to the flames, or it will melt.

You work for a little while, making a shield from the pail. You attach it. It looks like it just might do the trick. Now all you have to do is test it.

You paddle the board far out into the water. Then you start the rockets. They fire right up, and the surfboard goes shooting across the top of the water.

You grip the board tightly and ride it on top of the waves. When you see a big wave approach, you lean back, and fly right over it!

The farther you go out, the bigger the waves

get. You are caught up in the rush. You keep surfing and surfing and surfing . . .

Putt . . . putt . . . putt . . . putt . . .

The rockets stop. You check them out. The problem isn't the shield this time—it's the fuel tank. You've surfed so far, you're out of fuel.

No problem, you think. *I'll just paddle back in to shore.*

But when you turn the board around, you gasp. You can't even see Club Penguin!

"I'm lost at sea!" you wail.

There's nothing for you to do but paddle and hope you see land soon. But on the bright side, once you get there, Gary's going to be really proud of you!

THE END

You just can't wait.

"Gary, before we start, I've got to show you something," you say. "After I sent you those plans I actually designed my freeze ray. It's right here in my bag!"

You take the messenger bag off of your shoulder.

"Impressive!" Gary says. "However, remember that this prototype you have made is still highly experimental."

"Of course," you say, and your flippers are trembling with excitement. Gary is impressed!

You are so excited that you open the messenger bag upside down without realizing it. Your freeze ray falls out.

"Oh, no!" you cry. You reach out to grab it. But you're too late. The ray clatters to the floor.

Zap! An icy blast shoots from the ray. It hits Gary! Before you can turn off the ray, Gary is frozen solid.

At first, you can't believe what you are seeing. You reach out and gingerly touch Gary. He is ice cold. It looks like you have made an ice sculpture shaped like Gary—but you know it's really him.

For a quick second you're proud of yourself. Your freeze ray works!

Then panic sets in. You only tested it once before, on a pizza. That pizza is still back in your igloo, frozen solid.

What will happen to Gary? Will he stay frozen forever?

I've got to unfreeze him, fast! you think. You quickly run to the door of the Sport Shop and turn the "Open" sign to "Closed." If a penguin walked in and saw this, it would be terrible.

Then you take a deep breath and look at your ray. You designed your ray to unfreeze frozen things, too. But you have never tested the unfreezing ability of the ray. In fact, you're not even sure how it works.

You bring the freeze ray to Gary's desk and unscrew a tiny panel that opens up the inner compartment. There is a tangle of colored wires in there: yellow, green, red, and blue. Theoretically, the freezing will reverse if you switch around the wires that made Gary freeze.

Think, think, think, you tell yourself. You know the yellow and green wires work together. But so do the red and blue wires.

You know you need to switch two of the wires. But which two should you switch?

If you switch the red and blue wires, go to page 47.
If you switch the yellow and green wires, go to page 74.

CONTINUED FROM PAGE 19.

Your curiosity gets the best of you.

"Um, maybe I should stay here and watch the Sport Shop for you," you suggest.

"Excellent idea," Gary agrees. "This won't take long. When I return, we will commence with your apprenticeship."

Gary puts down his coffee and hurries out the door. Through the window, you watch him waddle down the path that leads to the Town Center and the Plaza.

You feel nervous. You won't touch anything, you promise yourself. And just one little peek won't hurt.

You're just not sure what to peek at first.

If you look under the tarp, go to page 61.
If you try to open the door marked "Gary's Room," go to page 80.

"I should really go find Gary," you decide. You start to walk across the Sport Shop when you realize you have a problem. Gary is all the way at the Plaza, in the Pizza Parlor. With your new teeny-tiny legs, it will take you forever to walk there! And you're not even sure you can push open the door by yourself.

Just then, the door swings open. A Tour Guide walks in. She's pink and wearing a cap with a question mark on it. Three penguins waddle in behind her. You quickly hide behind a soccer ball.

"Here in the Sport Shop, you will find the latest sports gear and clothing," the Guide is saying to her group.

Perfect! You can hitch a ride with her. With luck, she'll take her group to the Plaza.

"A new catalog is released about every two months," the Guide is saying. She has her back to you. You jump on to her sneaker and grab tightly on to the laces.

She leads the group out of the Sport Shop and down the snowy path to the Dock.

"Here at the Dock, you can play *Hydro-Hopper*," the Guide explains. You listen, trying to be patient. You will never get to the Plaza at this rate!

"Next stop, the Coffee Shop," the Guide says cheerfully. Thank goodness! At least you're headed into the Town Center.

You keep hanging on as she leads the group inside the Coffee Shop. The red stuffed couches look like big mountains. The coffee counter looks like a skyscraper.

"Let's go upstairs. I'll teach you how to play *mancala*," says the Guide.

That is one detour you don't want to take. You hop off the Tour Guide's sneaker. You will try to hitch a ride from another penguin.

You look up. A lime green penguin next to you is wearing a coat with big, soft pockets. He's standing next to a stack of newspapers.

"I sure could go for a slice of pizza," he is saying.

That's just where you need to go! You scramble up the stack. From there, you should be able to hop right into his pocket.

At that moment, another penguin comes in

and grabs the newspaper out from under you.
You go flying.

"Aaaaaaah!" you scream, but you are so
small nobody hears you.

Go to page 13.

CONTINUED FROM PAGE 67.

You tell the penguin, "No, thanks!" and run to the Coffee Shop.

There it is—a green notebook on one of the tables. A server is about to pick it up.

"My friend Gary left that here," you tell him. "I'll bring it to him."

"Thanks!" the server says.

You can't believe your luck. You leave the Coffee Shop and head for your time machine. In your hurry, you bump into a penguin.

It's Gary—from the past! "I was just coming back to get my notebook, but I see you've found it for me. Thank you."

You don't know what to do. You are supposed to bring the notebook back to *future* Gary, aren't you? Should you give this Gary the notebook instead—or make a run for it?

If you quickly run to the time machine, go to page 68.
If you decide to try to explain things to Gary, go to page 59.

CONTINUED FROM PAGE 23.

Even though the heatproof shield is heavy, you think it's the best choice. Gary helps you attach it. Then the blue penguin in the jet pack flies you back to the Cove.

Soon you are dangling over the blue ocean waves.

"Ready?" he asks you.

You turn on the rockets. "Ready!" you answer.

Then he drops you. The surfboard is charged up and ready to go. You land on top of a crest of water and ride the wave.

It's awesome! The wave drops underneath your board, and you do a backflip, landing safely on the water below. The extra power from the rockets makes doing the trick easier. Confident, you decide to try a double backflip.

"Cowabunga!" you cry. Then you steer the board over the waves. One . . . two . . . *splash!* You made it!

"All right!" The rockets make surfing more fun than ever. You try some more tricks. You do a handstand on the board and try a coastal kick, dancing while you're upside down. It's a little tricky to do at superspeed. You decide to stick to flipping.

It's a good decision. You soar over the waves, flipping backward and forward. After an amazing triple flip, you paddle the board back to shore.

Some penguins crowd around you. "That was awesome!" they say. "Where did you get that board?"

"Sorry. That's top secret," you tell them. Then you hurry back to the Sport Shop.

Gary is very pleased with your report.

"I could use a helpful penguin like you around here," he says. "I am not quite ready for an official assistant yet. Perhaps someday. In the meantime, I'd like to call on you from time to time to help me test out new inventions."

"That would be great!" you say. Helping out Gary is a dream come true!

THE END

CONTINUED FROM PAGE 16.

You press the round button.

Zap! The machine shoots out another laser. You dive off the shoe box to make sure the beam hits you.

Your body starts to tingle once more. You watch, thrilled, as your body begins to grow. Soon you're back to normal size.

But your body is still tingling, and you keep growing. Soon, you're taller than the machine. Then your head starts to graze the ceiling of the Sport Shop. Luckily, you're thinking clearly. You quickly run outside the door.

You keep growing . . . and growing . . . and growing. You don't stop until you're taller than the top of the two-story Sport Shop. You're so tall, you can see the top of the Ski Hill!

"Hello up there!"

You look down to see Gary standing at your very big feet. A small crowd of penguins has gathered nearby, too.

"Hi, Gary!" you call down. "I, um, got into a little bit of trouble."

"Looks like a *big* bit of trouble to me,"

Gary says, chuckling. "Let me retrieve the Size-a-Tron 3000."

Gary goes inside the shop and comes out dragging the machine. He points the laser at you and pushes the big button. A green beam flashes quickly, and then burns out. Gary frowns. He examines the machine for a moment.

"There appears to be a malfunction," Gary says. "Fortunately, it's fixable. We should have you back to normal in a few days."

"A few days!" you wail. "What am I going to do?"

Gary smiles. "I would suggest ordering your pizzas with *extra* cheese," he jokes.

THE END

CONTINUED FROM PAGE 19.

You remind yourself you're here to learn from Gary. Besides, you love pizza too much to let the Pizzatron 3000 stay broken.

"Of course I'll go with you," you say.

You and Gary hurry to the Pizza Parlor. When you enter, a blast of warm air from the pizza ovens greets you. Relaxing piano music plays. But the candlelit tables are all empty.

The Pizza Parlor manager rushes over to greet you.

"Gary, I'm so glad you're here!" he says. "The conveyor belt on the Pizzatron 3000 has stopped moving. I can't make any more pizzas. If you can't get the machine working, I'll have to close the shop!"

"It sounds like a simple malfunction," Gary tells him. "Let me see the machine."

You follow Gary and the manager through the beaded curtain leading to the kitchen. The Pizzatron 3000 has come to a dead stop.

The main part of the machine is a tall metal box with an on/off switch. From there, pizza dough is dropped onto the conveyor belt.

Toppings like sauce and seaweed are added. Then the finished pizzas drop off of the conveyor belt and are delivered to customers.

"I will examine the motor," Gary says. He points to a gear box underneath the conveyor belt. "The levers are in the wrong starting position. Can you reset them correctly for me?"

You realize that Gary is talking to you.

"Sure," you say. You look down at the box.

There are five levers attached to the box: two red ones, two green ones, and a blue one. You see that all five levers are pushed in. You know that some of them should be pulled out—you're just not sure which ones.

Gary starts to tinker with the motor, and you start to sweat. You must have made a million pizzas using the Pizzatron 3000, but you can't remember which levers to pull out. But you do know it's *not* the blue lever . . .

If you pull the two red levers forward, go to page 51.
If you pull the two green levers forward, go to page 69.

CONTINUED FROM PAGE 14.

You know you can't dodge all those dancing feet, so you hop on the first shoe you see—a glittery Stardust Slipper. You hang on to the strap, but it's hard to get a good grip as the dancing penguin starts to boogie. Thankfully, she leaves the Night Club. Her slippers crunch on the snow as she heads down to the path.

"Please go to the Plaza. Go to the Plaza," you whisper. Soon you see towering walls of snow and realize you're in the Snow Forts. Almost there!

Suddenly, the penguin breaks into a run. You lose your grip and fall off the slipper into the snow. You look up and see she is running away from a snowball fight.

"Hey, wait for me!" you call out, but you know she can't hear you. Before you can dust off the snow, you see a shadow above you. A red penguin reaches down to grab some snow. He grabs you with the snow and packs you into a big snowball.

"Help! Help!" you yell, but it's no use. The red penguin tosses you into the air.

"Aaaaaaaaaaaaah!" You go flying across the forts and crash into the target powering the Club Penguin Clock Tower, falling to the ground. The snow around you is soft, and you're not hurt.

"Bull's-eye!" the red penguin shouts.

You dust off the snow once more and take in the situation. The red penguin has run off. A purple penguin and a green penguin are having a snowball fight. You should probably hitch a ride with one of them. But which one?

If you hitch a ride on the purple penguin, go to page 27.
If you hitch a ride on the green penguin, go to page 49.

CONTINUED FROM PAGE 33.

You decide to switch the red and blue wires. You make the change and close the compartment. Then you point the freeze ray at Gary and fire.

Poof! There are sparks from the freeze ray. You have broken it!

You jump into panic mode again. You start fiddling with the freeze ray. You switch the yellow and green, the red and yellow, the blue and green—but nothing works. Your freeze ray is fried.

Think like a scientist, you tell yourself. You can't unfreeze Gary with your ray. So you need to try another method. What's another way to unfreeze something?

"Heat," you say out loud. You think it through. If you put Gary next to something hot, like a fire, he could melt. It could work.

Or it could go terribly wrong. What if Gary himself turns into a puddle?

You wish you had someone to talk to. Advice . . . you need advice.

That's it! You can ask Aunt Arctic what

to do. She's great at giving advice. But will Gary be more impressed if you solve the problem yourself? It could be worth the risk.

If you decide to bring Gary to the Ski Lodge fireplace, go to page 71.
If you ask Aunt Arctic what to do, go to page 56.

CONTINUED FROM PAGE 46.

You jump on the boot of the green penguin. The purple penguin waves and waddles off. The green penguin stands there.

"What should I do next?" he wonders.

You're not taking any chances. "Some pizza would be nice about now," you call up.

The penguin looks around. "Who said that?" he asks. Then he shrugs. "You know, some pizza *would* be good right now."

The green penguin heads right for the Pizza Parlor. You're relieved as soon as he steps inside. You hang on until he's in front of the counter. Then you hop off his boot. You run over to the beaded curtain leading inside the kitchen. You duck as one of the beads almost hits you in the head.

In front of you is a box of gears with levers on it. You recognize it. It's the bottom of the Pizzatron 3000! You look around and see Gary's foot in the distance.

"Finally!" you cheer.

You run toward it. Then you jump up and pull on the bottom of Gary's lab coat.

"Gary! Gary! Down here!" you yell.

Gary looks down. He takes off his eyeglasses and cleans the lenses with the sleeve of his jacket. Then he puts his glasses back on.

"Aha!" he says. "You have discovered the Size-a-Tron 3000."

"How'd you guess?" you ask.

Gary reaches down and gently picks you up. Surprisingly, he doesn't seem upset. "What a nice surprise. I am glad to see my new invention works. And the timing is perfect! I happen to need a penguin just your size right now."

Go to page 55.

You pull out the two red levers.

"I think I've cleared a jam in the motor—" Gary starts to say.

That's when things go wrong.

The conveyor belt starts to chug along at superspeed. Tomato sauce and hot sauce shoot out of the containers. Cheese flies up in the air and sprinkles down like rain. You duck as a squid flies past your head.

Gary steps out from behind the machine, when *SPLAT!* an anchovy lands on his eyeglass lens.

"We appear to have a malfunction," Gary says calmly. He walks to the gear box, ignoring the pizza sauce splattering all over his jacket. He pushes in the two red levers and pulls out the two green levers. The machine calms down.

"Sorry, Gary," you say. "I pulled the wrong levers."

"The fault is mine," he says. "When I built this machine, I custom-calibrated the speed. That just means the conveyor belt moves at different speeds that can be controlled by the penguin operating it. I should have told you what speed it was set to before I sent you in!"

You're not sure what Gary has just said, but you're relieved he's not upset. He puts a flipper around your shoulder.

"You know, you remind me of when I was just starting out," he said. "I was working on a snow-cone flavoring machine and ended up smelling like raspberries for a month—all because I didn't correctly tighten the valve for the output tubing!" Gary chuckles, and you laugh along with him—even though you're not quite sure you get the joke.

"Let's sit down and share a pizza," Gary suggests. "I'd like to get your ideas about a problem I've been having with a prototype sled I've been working on. It falls apart every time I take it out for a test run."

"Great!" you reply. Pizza and a one-on-one with Gary? It sounds like a perfect day to you!

THE END

You just can't keep the secret.

"You're right," you whisper to her. "It's a new invention, and it's top secret. It's a rocket-powered surfboard!"

Your friend's eyes get wide. "Whoa. Can you play *Catchin' Waves* with it?"

You nod. "Yup. I'm about to test it out."

"Oh, you've got to let me ride with you!" your friend says.

"I'm not sure," you say. "This is a scientific test."

"Oh pleeeeeeease," your friend pleads. "This is a once-in-a-lifetime chance. And I'm an excellent surfer. I can help you."

Your friend makes a good argument.

"All right," you say. "Let's go."

You head back to the Surf Hut on the shore. The blue penguin in the jet pack gives you a funny look when he sees you and your friend holding the surfboard together.

"It's part of the test," you explain.

The blue penguin shrugs. "Okay, then."

He picks up you and your friend and

carries you over the water. This time, you turn on the rockets before he drops you.

"Let's do it!" you cry.

Splash! The surfboard slams into the water. You and your friend try to balance, but you're too heavy for the speeding board.

The surfboard tumbles upside down. You try to hold on, but lose your grip. When you get your head above water, you're relieved to see your friend is okay. But one thing is missing.

"Oh, no!" you wail. "Where's the board?"

"It must have been carried away by a wave," your friend says.

You swim back to shore. How are you going to explain to Gary that you lost the board? Well, at least you tested it for him . . .

THE END

CONTINUED FROM PAGE 50.

"There is a loose wire inside the Pizzatron 3000 that I am not able to reach," Gary explains. "Can you please connect it for me?"

"I'll try," you reply. Gary places you on a metal rod inside the machine.

"It's the blue wire," he says.

You walk across the rod like it's a tightrope. Then you grab on to a red wire and swing like Tarzan over to another rod. You reconnect the blue wire. Then you reverse the whole process until you're back in Gary's steady flipper.

"Great job," Gary says. "Let me get you back to the Sport Shop and return you to normal size."

"Hey, before we do that, how about a pizza?" you suggest.

"Excellent idea!" Gary agrees.

Soon you're standing on a table with a pizza the size of a football field in front of you—and it's all yours! Even better, you're hanging out with Gary. It's like a dream come true!

THE END

CONTINUED FROM PAGE 48.

You decide that talking to Aunt Arctic is the smartest thing to do. You hurry off to her igloo.

Aunt Arctic opens the door and smiles at you. She looks just like her picture in *The Club Penguin Times*: a green penguin with a friendly face, black eyeglasses, and a pink hat on her head. A pencil is tucked into her eyeglass frames.

"Why hello," she says. "May I help you?"

"I froze Gary the Gadget Guy!" you blurt.

"Sounds like there's a story here—fill me in," Aunt Arctic says.

You follow her into her cozy igloo. The room is filled with puffles of every color. Some are napping on the orange rug in front of the fireplace.

"It happened like this," you begin. Then you tell her your story.

"Hmm," Aunt Arctic says. "You know, a nice hot beverage from the Coffee Shop always thaws me out when I'm feeling chilly."

"Coffee! That just might work," you say. "Thank you."

You rush to the Coffee Shop and order a cup of joe to go. Then you race back to the Sport Shop. It's still warm when you get there. You put the cup up to Gary's icy beak.

The steam from the cup starts to melt the ice! Gary starts to sip the coffee. The warmth flows through his body, and the rest of the ice melts in puddles around his feet.

"I say," Gary says. "That freeze ray of yours really works!"

The shop door opens, and Aunt Arctic waddles in.

"Glad to see you've warmed up, Gary," she says. Then she whips out a notebook. "Mind if I write about this for *The Club Penguin Times*?"

"Of course not," Gary says, and you're thrilled. You're going to be in the news!

THE END

CONTINUED FROM PAGE 20.

You press the square button.

Zap! The machine shoots out another laser, and you dive off the shoe box to make sure the beam hits you.

Your body starts to tingle. You keep your eyes open, and see that you are growing! Soon you are back to normal size.

"Cool!" you say.

"What do we have here?"

You turn and see Gary in the doorway.

"Gary, I can explain," you say.

"I understand," Gary says. "It is natural for a scientist to be curious. However, I was planning to demonstrate the machine for you as a surprise. Since you've already seen it, there is no reason to continue your apprenticeship."

You're a little disappointed, but that doesn't last long. After all, it's pretty sweet that you were turned into a tiny penguin with Gary's shrink ray. You can't wait to tell your friends!

THE END

CONTINUED FROM PAGE 38.

You decide to explain things to Gary. After all, he's Gary! He'll know what to do.

"I need to show you something," you say. Curious, Gary follows you to the time machine.

"This looks like a time machine!" Gary says. "I have been trying to figure out how to invent one for years."

"You do," you say. "You invent this in the future. Then you send me back in time to test it out—and to find your notebook for you. I'm just not sure about the notebook. Should I give it to you, or bring it back to the future?"

Gary is inside the time machine, studying the tubes with interest. "If I am going to build this time machine, I had better get back to work immediately," he says. "Take the notebook back to my future self. I'll be too busy working on the time machine to think about anything else!"

"Sounds good," you say.

Gary busily takes notes. Then he tears out the pages and hands the notebook to you.

"Best of luck on your journey," Gary says. You step inside the machine.

"See you in the future!" you say. Then you close the curtain and pull the lever.

The lights glow, the tunnel appears, and seconds later you are back in Gary's office, safe and sound.

"It's very odd!" Gary says. "Suddenly, I remember meeting you that day outside the Coffee Shop."

Thinking about it makes your brain hurt a little. You hand the notebook to Gary.

"You said to give this back to you," you say.

"Thank you," Gary says. "Now I can begin my latest invention. I would like to extend your apprenticeship. Can you help me work on it?"

You smile. "Of course!"

THE END

CONTINUED FROM PAGE 34.

The Sport Shop is empty. You go to the big blue tarp. You look both ways. Then you lift up the tarp.

"What is this?" you wonder out loud. The machine looks like a big metal box. There is an arm attached to the front, and some kind of tube extends from the arm. A control panel has rows of different-shaped buttons on it.

Now you are more curious than ever. There is no writing on the machine to explain what it is or what it does. You promised yourself you wouldn't touch anything. But if you don't press one of those buttons, you'll never learn about the machine.

You can't seem to help yourself. You reach forward and press the biggest button. The machine starts to hum.

"Whoa," you say.

The mechanical arm swings toward you. A green light glows from inside the tube. Then you hear a sizzling sound.

Zap!

Your whole body tingles. You have been

zapped with some kind of laser light from the tube! The bright light blinds you for a few seconds.

You slowly start to focus. In front of you, you see the machine—the very bottom of the machine. Right now, it looks like it's fifty feet tall!

"Wow! The machine grew!" you say.

Then you notice your voice sounds kind of squeaky. Something doesn't feel right. You slowly look around the room.

Everything in the room looks giant! You see a football nearby that looks twice as big as you are. The exercise machine is as big as a castle igloo.

"Uh, the Sport Shop got really big," you say hopefully, but deep down, you know the truth.

The Sport Shop did not get big.

You are really, really small!

Wow, you think. *I can't believe Gary invented a shrink ray. How did he manage to do that?*

Then reality hits you.

Gary didn't want you to see the machine. But you not only saw it, you used it. You disobeyed Gary. And now you are smaller than a puffle.

Think, you tell yourself. *There has to be a way out of this.*

You look up at the machine. There are a lot of buttons up there. If one of the buttons made you small, another one *should* make you big. You could make yourself big, cover the machine up with the tarp, and Gary would never know. There are two problems with that plan. One, the buttons won't be easy to reach. And two, when you do reach them, you won't know which one to push.

Or, you could find Gary and get him to help you. There are two problems with that plan, too. First, you'll have to get to the Pizza Parlor to find him. And then, of course, you'll have to tell him what you did. You're pretty sure he won't be happy.

You take a deep breath. You have to try *something*. You don't want to stay small forever!

If you decide to try the buttons, go to page 20.
If you go find Gary, go to page 35.

CONTINUED FROM PAGE 23.

You decide to go with the lightweight shield.
Gary helps you attach it to the surfboard. Then
the blue jet-pack penguin carries you to the Cove.

He drops you into the water. You turn on the
rockets. The surfboard surges across the waves.

"Oh, yeah!" you cheer. You stand up on the
board. You're about to attempt a backflip when
you hear a sputtering sound. You look behind you.

"Oh, no!" you say. The shield has melted.
The rocket flames are dying out.

Then you look in front of you. "OH, NO!"
you say louder as a giant wave slams into you!

The next thing you see is a yellow penguin
in a lifeguard shirt leaning over you. You realize
you are on the shore. You quickly sit up.

"Thanks!" you say to the lifeguard. "Did
you see my surfboard?"

The lifeguard points to the surfboard,
twisted and broken next to you. You groan. But
you don't think Gary will be too upset. After all,
it was just part of the test.

THE END

CONTINUED FROM PAGE 75.

You know you missed some great Club Penguin parties and events, and you'd love to see them.

"I'd like to go back to the past," you say.

"Excellent choice," Gary agrees. "In that case, I have a special task for you. Some time ago, I was in the Coffee Shop working on plans for a new invention. When I left the shop, I absentmindedly left my notebook behind. When I returned to look for it, it was gone.

"I would like to send you back to the very day I lost that notebook. I need you to go to the Coffee Shop and retrieve it for me."

"Will do!" you say. He opens the curtain and you step inside. The walls are lined with twisting tubes filled with neon-colored liquid. There is a lever hanging down from the ceiling.

"I will send you back in time to approximately thirty minutes before I left the Coffee Shop," Gary says. "After you retrieve the notebook, come back to the machine and pull the lever."

"Roger," you say. You are so excited.

Gary closes the curtain, and the machine begins to shake. The liquid in the tubes glows brightly. There is a faint buzzing in your ears. The next thing you see is a strange tunnel of dim light opening up in front of you, out of nowhere. Without warning, you feel yourself being sucked inside!

You blink and see that everything is quiet and calm. You open the curtain and step outside.

You are in the Town Center! The machine seems to have worked. Then you notice a group of penguins walking past you. They are all wearing red-and-orange Hawaiian leis.

"Hey, where did you get those?" you ask.

"They're free down at the Dock," one of the penguins replies.

"Can you believe it?" says another penguin. "It's the middle of winter, and there's a big luau going on!"

The Winter Luau of 2006! You've heard about it and read about it. You always wished you could go.

"We're heading back to the Dock right now," says one of the penguins. "Do you want to come with us?"

Gary did say you had thirty minutes to get the notebook. That's plenty of time to dash to the Dock and get a free lei—isn't it?

If you go straight to the Coffee Shop, go to page 38.
If you dash to the Dock, go to page 78.

CONTINUED FROM PAGE 38.

Running into Gary from the past shakes you up a bit. You've read about time travel and you know you're not supposed to mess with the space-time continuum—whatever that is. So you run.

"Sorry!" you cry. You bolt for the time machine. In your hurry, you trip and fall into the snow.

The notebook falls into an icy puddle. You pick it up and dodge into the time machine. You quickly close the curtain, pull the lever, and *bam*! You're back in the future.

You open the curtain and see you're back in the Sport Shop. Gary looks thrilled.

"It worked!" he says. "And you have my notebook."

You hand him the dripping notebook. He opens it up, and the pencil marks inside are smeared from the water. His notes are ruined!

"No matter," Gary says. "The time machine works. We can send you back again to get it right."

You hope you do the right thing this time!

THE END

A drop of sweat rolls down your face. You close your eyes and try to picture what the Pizzatron 3000 looks like before you start making pizzas. And then it comes to you.

You confidently reach forward and pull the two green levers toward you. You hear the hum of a motor. The conveyor belt starts to move.

Gary peeks out from behind the machine.

"A piece of stray seaweed got jammed in the motor," he reports. "And you have the levers correctly placed. Excellent!"

A round of pizza dough drops onto the conveyor belt. The manager quickly steps in front of you.

"I'll take it from here," he says. "One spicy pizza with squid coming up!"

He makes the pizza and turns to Gary. "How can I ever thank you?"

"Some pizza might be nice," Gary says. He looks at you. "I like extra cheese and anchovies on mine. How about you?"

"Sounds delicious!" you say.

You take your pizzas back to the Sport

Shop and eat them at Gary's desk. He swallows the last bite and wipes his beak with a napkin.

"You have a knack for mechanical things," Gary says.

"Thank you," you say. You feel so proud!

Gary stands up. "I think I may have been incorrect before. You may be just the penguin I need to help me with my new invention."

Gary walks to the blue tarp and gives it a yank. The tarp falls to the floor. Underneath is a plain white surfboard. It doesn't look especially interesting.

Then you notice the rockets attached to it.

"Whoa. Is that a *rocket-powered* surfboard?" you ask.

Go to page 10.

CONTINUED FROM PAGE 48.

You want to impress Gary. And you're
pretty sure Gary is frozen under a layer of ice.
That means just the ice will melt—not Gary.

There is a fireplace in the Ski Lodge right
next door. You try to pick up Gary, but he's
pretty heavy. You grab a surfboard from the
rack and push Gary onto it. Then you pick up
the rope attached to the board and pull Gary
across the floor.

It's not easy to get Gary to the Ski Lodge.
First you have to go down the stairs of the
Sport Shop. Gary slides off the board, and you
have to push him back up again. Then you have
to drag him across the snow, past the Tour
Guide booth, and up the stairs of the Ski Lodge.

It doesn't take long for a small crowd of
curious penguins hanging out at the Lodge to
gather around you. They are full of questions,
but you politely explain you're in the middle
of an emergency. You pull Gary over to the
fireplace.

It only takes a few minutes for the ice to
melt. You're relieved when you see Gary

underneath. He's a little soggy, but he's as good as new.

"Gary! You're all right!" you say happily.

Gary shivers. "What a fascinating test! I must get back to my lab to see what effects the freeze ray has had on my body. Congratulations on making such an interesting invention. It's too bad we'll have to cut your apprenticeship short."

"Sure, Gary. I understand," you say. But you're sad. You had a great opportunity to work with Gary, and now it's over! Oh, well. At least he is impressed with your invention!

Gary hurries out of the Sport Shop. You're about to head back to your igloo when a red penguin slips in the puddle of water in front of the fireplace. You reach down and help him up.

"Hey! What's that puddle doing there?" the penguin asks.

"It's my fault," you say glumly. "I accidentally froze Gary the Gadget Guy with my freeze ray, and then I had to melt him."

"No way! Did you win the Invention Contest?" the red penguin asks. "I love inventing things."

You and the red penguin take a seat by the fireplace and talk. It turns out you have a lot in common. You feel pretty good. You may have lost your chance to learn some of Gary's secrets, but at least you made a new friend!

THE END

You decide to switch the yellow and green wires. You carefully make the switch. Then you close up the compartment and waddle over to Gary.

"Here goes," you say. You aim the ray at him and turn it on.

Zap! This time, a red light shoots from the freeze ray.

It works! Gary quickly unfreezes. A puddle of water forms at his feet.

Gary adjusts his eyeglasses. "Fascinating!" he says. "I could certainly use a cup of coffee to warm me up."

"You're not mad?" you ask, relieved.

"The foundation of invention is trial and error," Gary says. "I am happy to be a test subject in the name of science. And now, perhaps you can return the favor for me."

"Anything you say, Gary," you reply.

"Excellent," Gary says. He waddles over to the back wall of the Sport Shop, and you follow him. Blueprints of Gary's inventions are tacked to the wall. He stops next to a big object hidden under a blue tarp. He pulls it off, and there is a tall metal box underneath. A curtain covers the opening. It almost looks like one of those booths at an arcade that you enter to get your picture taken.

"What *is* that?" you ask.

"This is the Time Machine 3000," Gary says proudly. "I have been working on it for quite a long time. But I need help testing it. I can work the machine, but I need someone to do the actual time traveling."

"Ooh, me, me, me!" you say, waving your flipper.

"Then I shall let you decide," Gary says. "Would you like to visit the future, or the past?"

You have to think about that. If you go to the past, you'll get to see things on Club Penguin that you have missed. But if you go to the future, you may get a glimpse of parties and games before any other penguin around.

If you go to the future, go to page 24.
If you go to the past, go to page 65.

It's top secret.

You can't forget Gary's words.

"New invention? What new invention?" you say quickly. "Gotta go."

You quickly paddle out as far as you can. Then you turn to look at the rockets once more. It probably makes sense to get the rockets going before a wave comes, you guess. You steady yourself with one flipper, and with the other, you flip the switch.

Vroooooooom! You're off! The surfboard goes shooting across the waves at superspeed.

"Woo hoo!" you cry out. You love playing *Catchin' Waves*, and this is like a supercharged version. You stand up and carefully balance yourself on the board. A wave comes toward you, and you sail right over the top of it.

"Yeah!" you cheer. You decide to try out a simple trick. You wave. You dance. As another wave approaches, you decide to jump over it. You lean back, ready to soar, when . . .

Putt . . . putt . . . putt . . . putt . . .

The rockets sputter out. You wipe out and

tumble into the water. You grab the board and paddle back to a secluded spot onshore.

Why did the rockets go out? You check, and the fuel tank is full.

The splashing water must have put out the rocket fire, you realize. You stand up. You'll have to go back and give Gary your report.

Then you get an idea. What if you try to fix the surfboard yourself? Gary will surely be impressed!

If you take the surfboard back to Gary, go to page 23.
If you try to fix the surfboard yourself to impress Gary, go to page 29.

"Sure," you tell the penguin. "I'll come, but we have to be quick! I have to be somewhere."

You rush down to the Dock as fast as you can. You take your lei and put it on. You are so happy! You can't wait to show your friends when you get back home. You tell the group of penguins thanks and hurry off.

You are heading back to the Coffee Shop when you hear some festive Hawaiian music. *I still have plenty of time,* you think. So you head toward the sound. You see a bunch of penguins playing limbo! You always wanted to dance under a pole and see how low you can go. A little limbo won't slow you down . . .

But you get caught up in the excitement of the party. By the time you remember your mission, it's too late. You run to the Coffee Shop and don't see Gary there. You flag down a waiter.

"Excuse me, was Gary the Gadget Guy just here?" you ask.

"Sure was," the penguin replies.

"Did you see him leave a notebook behind?" you ask.

"Gary already came back and asked me," the waiter reports. "We looked everywhere, but it's not here."

You feel terrible. You have failed your mission! You head back to the time machine—but it's gone!

You notice some penguins nearby.

"Hey, did you see a big machine sitting here?" you ask.

"Yeah, it was weird," one of them answers. "Some pink penguin stepped inside and a few seconds later, it vanished!"

You groan. Someone else is using the time machine. You are trapped in the past!

Maybe it won't be so bad. You'll get to do a lot of things that you missed. You just hope that somebody will take care of your puffle, Einstein, while you're gone.

THE END

CONTINUED FROM PAGE 34.

The Sport Shop is empty. You decide to make your move. You quickly go to the door. You turn the handle . . .

Beep! Beep! Beep! Beep!

A loud alarm wails through the shop. Red lights start to flash. The door opens—and Gary is behind it!

He presses a button on the wall, and the alarms and lights stop.

"The work I do for Club Penguin is very important," he says. "I did not really get a call from the Pizza Parlor. I wanted to see what you would do if you were left alone. You are an excellent inventor. But I need an apprentice I can trust. I am very sorry."

You groan. You had one chance to learn from Gary—and you blew it!

THE END